VERY EASY GUITAR TUNES

Anthony Marks

Designed by Doriana Berkovic

Edited by Jenny Tyler

Illustrated by Simone Abel
and Kim Blundell

Music selected, arranged and edited by Anthony Marks
New compositions by Anthony Marks
Guitar advisor: Mark Marrington
Music setting: Andrew Jones

About this book

You will already know some of these tunes, though others might be less familiar. Some of them were written specially for this book. If you have a computer, you can listen to all the tunes on the Usborne Quicklinks Website to hear how they go. Just go to **www.usborne-quicklinks.com** and enter the keywords "very easy guitar tunes", then follow the simple instructions.

At the start of every piece there is a picture in a circle. Each picture has a sticker to match it in the middle of the book. Use the stickers to show when you have learned a piece.

Contents

Guitar reminders

Here are some hints to help you enjoy guitar playing more. You can read these first, or go straight to the music on page 4 and come back here if you want some reminders.

If you need to know the fingering for a particular note, there is a chart on page 32 showing how to play all the notes in this book.

Getting comfortable

When you play the guitar, it is important to feel relaxed so that your fingers can move easily. Experiment until you find a position that feels right for you. At first, it will probably feel easiest to rest the guitar on your right leg, as shown below.

When you are used to playing, you may want to try resting the guitar on your left leg (see below). Raise your left leg slightly (you can use a special support for this). This position makes it easier to see your hands and fingers by leaning forward slightly.

Rest your right arm on top of the guitar.

Make sure the guitar is upright (not sloping forwards or backwards).

The guitar neck should be level or pointing slightly upwards.

Keep your back straight but not stiff.

Sit on the front part of the chair.

Support for your left foot

Left hand and fingers

Hold your left thumb straight out. Place it on the back of the guitar neck, about in line with the second fret.
 Curve your fingers over the strings so that when you press them down your fingertips are at right angles to the strings.

Press the strings firmly just to the left of the fretwire.

Your fingernails need to be fairly short.

Keep your hand and wrist relaxed

Don't press too hard.

Plucking the strings

For the tunes in this book, you can pluck the strings in different ways. You can use the fingers and thumb of your right hand, or you can use a small piece of plastic called a plectrum or pick.
 If you use your fingers, begin by plucking the strings with your index and middle fingers. Keep them fairly straight and try to alternate between them. (This is known as rest stroke.) Rest your

thumb gently on the sixth string to keep your hand steady. Later on in the book, some of the pieces tell you to play the lower notes with your thumb.
 If you are using a plectrum, hold it between your first finger and thumb. Move your wrist to play the strings. You can pluck the string in both directions - towards your face and away from it.

Au clair de la lune

This tune was written in France in the 17th century. The title means "By the light of the moon."

Merrily we roll along

This is an old American song. It is also the same tune as the nursery rhyme "Mary had a little lamb". Nobody knows which came first.

La capucine

"La capucine" is a French nursery rhyme from the 18th century. "Capucine" is French for "nasturtium", a kind of flower.

Highland laddie

This tune was written specially for this book. When you know it well, try playing it fast, then slow. Which sounds best?

Fais dodo

This is an old French lullaby. "Dodo" is a childish word for "sleep", so "Fais dodo" means "Go to sleep". During the rest, use your right-hand finger or thumb to stop the G string from sounding. This is called damping.

Learning new tunes

It helps to learn each new tune slowly and carefully. First, clap the rhythm as you count the beats. Then, when you know the rhythm, try playing the notes.

Keep going to the end of the tune and don't worry if you play wrong notes. You can always go back and try it again afterwards.

Happy as a lark

Can you think of ways to make this tune sound happy? For the note C, use string 2, fret 1, finger 1.

Pease pudding hot

Pease pudding is made of peas and bacon. It was popular in medieval times, when this song was first sung. Look out for the rests in this tune, and try damping the string with your right hand finger or thumb.

Summer's here

This tune was written specially for this book. Play it smoothly and try not to rush. For the note D, use string 2, fret 3, finger 3.

À la claire fontaine

This is a Canadian tune. Its title is French for "By the clear fountain". French people first went to live in Canada in the 17th century.

Go and tell Aunt Nancy

This is an old American folk tune. You will need the notes G, A, B, C and D, so try these out a few times before you start to play.

The snow goose

This tune was written specially for this book. Try playing it in different ways. Does it sound better fast or slow? Loud or quiet?

Getting ready to play

Each time you begin playing, it's a good idea to exercise your fingers gently. You can do this by playing scales. A scale is a line of notes that goes up and down by step. On the right is a scale of all the notes you have used so far. Play it a few times to warm your fingers up and get them ready to play tunes.

London Bridge is falling down

London Bridge had to be rebuilt many times because the River Thames kept sweeping it away. Look out for high E (open string 1) in this tune.

Give me your hand

"Give me your hand" is an old English folk tune. Make sure you hold the last note for three full beats.

Don't forget!

When you are playing, remember to sit up straight and keep your guitar upright.

Keep your thumb behind the neck and your left-hand fingers curled. And count the rhythm as you play - either out loud or in your head.

If you are using your right-hand fingers to pluck, don't forget to alternate between the index and middle fingers as you play.

Old Macdonald had a farm

You have to play shorter notes in this tune. They are called quavers or eighth notes. Count carefully, and make sure you don't rush.

Lavender's blue

This is an old English folk tune. Look out for the jumps between the G string and the E string in the pieces on these pages. Make sure you don't hit the B string on your way past.

Mattachins

"Mattachins" is an old French sword dance. Don't play it too quickly. You have to count two beats in each bar.

New notes on string 1

Try the notes F and G on string 1 a few times to get used to them. For F, use finger 1, fret 1. For G, use finger 3, fret 3. Play the music below a few times to help you get used to these new notes. You can play this music while someone else plays "Mattachins". Count a few bars together before you start, so that you begin at the same time. You need to play the music below twice to fit with "Mattachins".

Goddesses

This is an old English folk tune. You need high G (string 1, fret 3, finger 3). Try this note a few times before you begin.

Old Joe Clark

This is an old American tune. You can play it on your own, or with another guitarist. Find out more below.

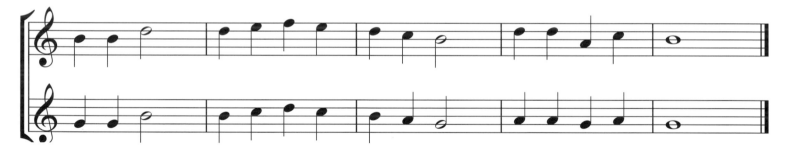

Tunes for two players

A tune for two players is called a duet. In a duet, one person plays the top line of music while someone else plays the lower one.

Before you try this, play your own part a few times until you know it well. (It can help to learn the other part too, so that you know what the other person is going to play.)

Then, when you play with someone else, count a few bars together before you start so that you begin at the same time. When you both know the music, try exchanging parts.

You could record one part and play the other over the top.

You can download duet parts from the Internet (see page 2).

Sur le pont d'Avignon

This is a French tune. The title means "On the bridge at Avignon", though people used to dance on an island in the river under the bridge, not on top of it.

Home on the range

This American tune was written in the 1870s. It begins on the last beat of the bar, so count a few bars before you start. Watch out for the ties, too.

For the ties, hold the first note for as long as both notes added together.

13

Streets of Laredo

This is an old cowboy tune. Laredo is a city in Texas, near the border between America and Mexico. You can play this as a duet (see page 12).

Michael Finnegan

Make the notes in this tune quite short and spiky, but don't play it too fast. At the beginning, count three beats, then start on the fourth.

Long, long ago

"Long, long ago" was written by Thomas Haynes Bayley, and first published in America in 1843. Look out for low D (open string 4).

O, du lieber Augustin

This is an old German folk tune. Its title means "My dear Augustin". In English it is sometimes known as "Buy a broom".

Row, row, row your boat

Try to play this smoothly and gently. Imagine you are rowing in a boat on a calm day. Don't rush the third beat of the bar, and watch out for the tied notes.

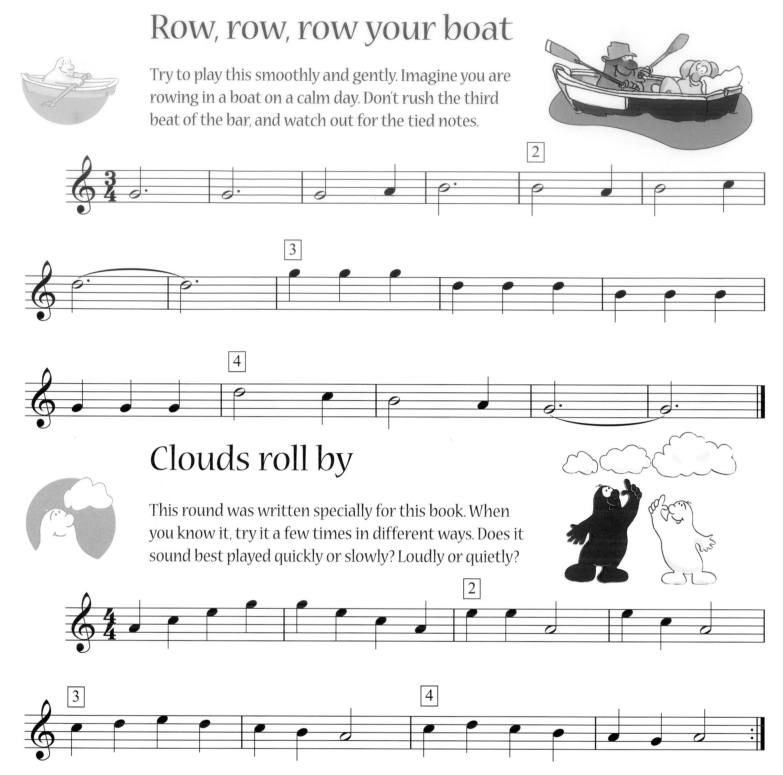

Clouds roll by

This round was written specially for this book. When you know it, try it a few times in different ways. Does it sound best played quickly or slowly? Loudly or quietly?

Rounds

A round is a tune that can be played by several people. All the tunes on these two pages are rounds. Each person starts a few bars apart, as shown by the numbers in boxes on the music.

When the first player gets to number 2, the second player starts at the beginning. When the first player gets to number 3, the third player starts, and so on. You have to decide how many times you are each going to play the tune, then stop one by one.

The tunes on this page can be played by up to four people, but they will work with two or three as well. If there is just you, they will work as solos too. If there are lots of you, more than one person can play each part.

Frère Jacques

The title of this old French song means "Brother James". It is about a monk who sleeps too late in the morning.

London's burning

People sang this tune after the Great Fire of London in 1666. The fire burned for five days and thousands of buildings were destroyed.

Jacques comes back!

This is a new tune that uses the same notes as "Frère Jacques," but not in the same order. Can you work out what has happened? You can still play it as a round.

What happens if you play backwards from the end?

Cornflowers

This tune was specially written for this book. Play it gently, and not too quickly. You will need new notes on string 4: E (fret 2, finger 2) and F (fret 3, finger 3).

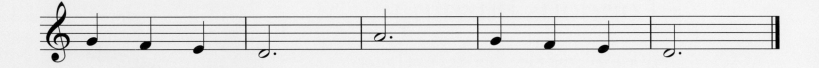

The ash grove

This is an old Welsh folk song. Play it smoothly and not too quickly. Watch out for low F.

Playing loudly and quietly

In the tunes on these pages, you will find signs telling you how loudly to play. You can see what these signs mean on the right. But remember they are only suggestions - try playing tunes in different ways and decide which you prefer.

To play loudly on the guitar, pluck the string a little harder. To play softly, pluck a little more gently.

This sign tells you to play loudly.

This sign tells you to play quietly.

Cornflowers too

"Cornflowers too" makes a duet with "Cornflowers" on the opposite page. Ask someone else to play it with you. Count a few bars together before you start.

Turn the glasses over

This is a sailor's song called a sea shanty. "Shanty" comes from the French word "chanter", which means "to sing".

Forest Green

Nobody knows who wrote this English Christmas carol, but it is hundreds of years old. Play it quietly, like a lullaby.

We wish you a merry Christmas

This English tune was written in the 19th century in the reign of Queen Victoria. This is also when Christmas cards were invented.

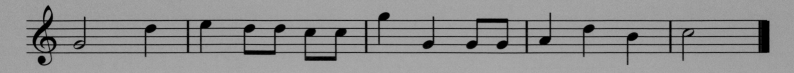

Hymn to joy

The German composer, Ludwig van Beethoven, wrote this in 1827. It is now the anthem of the European Union. Count the dotted notes carefully.

Wedding march

This tune was written in the 19th century by a German composer, Richard Wagner. It comes from an opera (a play with music) called "Lohengrin", and is played during a wedding scene.

All things bright and beautiful

The sharp sign at the beginning of the music is called a key signature. It tells you to play F sharp whenever you see the note F.

Hot cross buns

Hot cross buns are sweet bread rolls with a cross sign on the top of them. When market traders sold them they sang this tune to attract customers.

Benjamin Bowlabags

This tune was written in the 19th century. It is from Cornwall, in southwest England. It is also known as "The Proud Tailor".

Michael, row the boat ashore

This tune is a spiritual. Spirituals were first sung in America in the early 19th century. Play smoothly and evenly, as if you were floating in a boat.

Watch out for F sharp!

Song of the Volga boatmen

The Volga is a river in Russia. Sailors sang this as they rowed their boats. Make the music very rhythmic. Try playing it slowly, then quickly. Which sounds better?

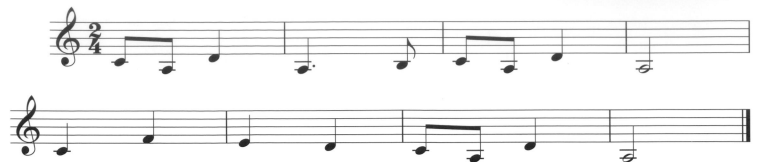

Duckling in the meadow

This is another Russian tune. Does it sound best fast or slow? Make the short notes smooth and even and try not to rush them.

New notes on string 5

The tunes on these pages use new notes on string 5. The note A is the open string, and you will also need B (finger 2, fret 2) and C (finger 3, fret 3).

These tunes can be played all the way through using just your right-hand thumb, or with just your right-hand fingers. Try them both ways. Which feels more comfortable? If you use your thumb for the lower strings, it may feel easier to change to your fingers if the tune moves up to higher strings.

In an English country garden

Look out for the repeat. Play the first section twice.

This is an old dance tune. When you know it well, try it a different way. In each group of two short notes, make the first a little longer than the second.

What shall we do with the drunken sailor?

This is a sea shanty. Sailors sang shanties while they pulled ropes, keeping time with the music. This made the work easier. As in the tune above, try playing the pairs of short notes unevenly. Which version do you prefer?

Johnny Todd

This is an English sea shanty. The flat sign at the beginning tells you to play B flat whenever you see the note B. Look out for the pause - hold this note a little longer than the others.

B flat is string 3, fret 3, finger 3.

Pause

Berloogy werloogy

This tune was written specially for this book. Play it very rhythmically. Look out for B flats, and one ordinary B.

Red river valley

This is an old cowboy song that was first sung in the American southwest in the 19th century.

Scarborough fair

This English tune was first sung in the Middle Ages. Once a year there was a huge market and fair in the seaside town of Scarborough.

Now is the month of Maying

An English composer, Thomas Morley, wrote this tune around 1595. He was the organist at Saint Paul's Cathedral in London. Look out for the repeat signs in this tune: you have to play each section twice.

High on the hills

This duet was written specially for this book.
The lower part uses notes on string 6: E (open),
F sharp (fret 2, finger 2) and G (fret 3, finger 3).

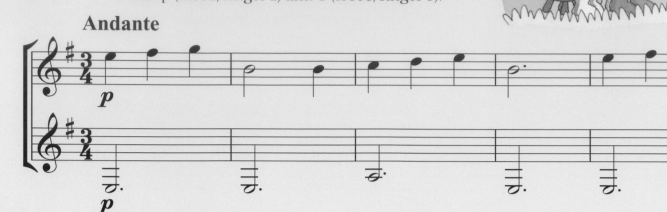

Don't forget
F sharp - it's in the
key signature!

Andante

Mockingbird

This is an old American tune. Make the short
notes very even and try not to rush. Look out
for G on string 6 (finger 3, fret 3).

Allegro

Land of the silver birch

This is a Canadian tune. Play it lightly and
evenly. Does it sound better fast or slow?
Try it both ways, then decide.

Morning has broken

Nobody knows who wrote this hymn tune.
It may be a folk song. Look out for bottom F
(string 6, fret 1, finger 1).

Moderato

mf

f

mf

29

Ding dong merrily on high

Although this tune is best known as a carol, it is a French dance from the 16th century. You can play it as a duet, or play the top line on your own.

Transposing

Below are two tunes from earlier in the book which you learned on strings 1, 2 and 3. Now their first lines are written out starting on lower strings. Can you play the rest of each tune? (Look at the fingering chart on page 32 if you get stuck!)

Moving a tune like this is called transposing. You could try transposing other tunes from earlier in the book yourself. It helps you to find your way around the guitar and to understand more about music.

Michael, row the boat ashore (page 23)

Scarborough fair (page 27)

The first Nowell

Follow the signs for loud and soft in this old English carol. Watch out for the repeat, too - you have to play the first section twice.

God rest ye merry, gentlemen

This Christmas song is very old, but it first became popular in England in the 19th century. Don't rush the short notes.

Notes in this book

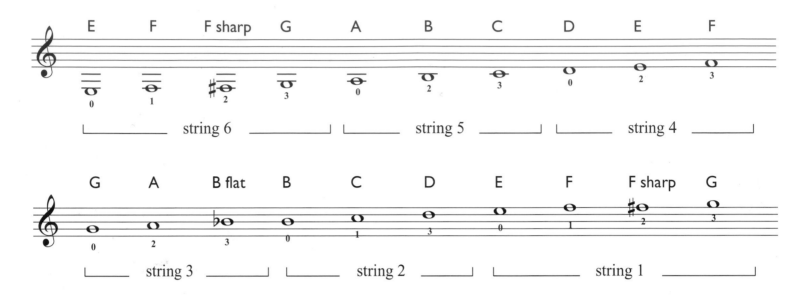

Below you can check how to play the notes used in this book. The staves show the notes and their names. The small numbers tell you which left-hand finger you normally use to play the note.

The symbol 0 means that the note is an open string - you don't use any left-hand fingers. Underneath the staves, the string numbers tell you which string to use - string 6 is low E, string 1 is high E.

Finding notes on the guitar

The diagram below shows you where to put your fingers to play all the notes in this book. On the left you will see the string numbers, and the note-names of each open string.

The frets show you where to put your left-hand fingers to play each note. Normally you use finger 1 for fret 1, finger 2 for fret 2 and finger 3 for fret 3.

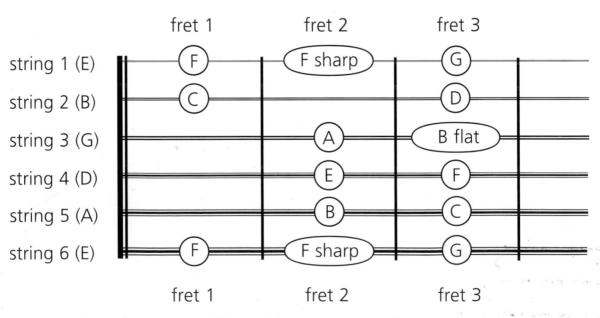